TWILIGHT

MOONBEAM ALLEY

STEFAN ZWEIG

TWILIGHT

MOONBEAM ALLEY

Translated from the German by Anthea Bell

PUSHKIN PRESS
LONDON

Original text © Williams Verlag AG. Zurich
Twilight first published in German
as *Geschichte eines Unterganges* in 1910
Moonbeam Alley first published in German
as *Die Mondscheingasse* in 1922

Translation copyright © Anthea Bell 2005

This edition first published in 2005 by
Pushkin Press
12 Chester Terrace
London NW1 4ND

British Library Cataloguing in Publication Data:
A catalogue record for this book is available
from the British Library

ISBN 1 901285 57 X

Cover *Figure in the Moonlight*
by John Atkinson Grimshaw (1836-93)

Frontispiece Stefan Zweig
© Roger-Viollet Rex Features

Jeanne Agnès Berthelot de Plémont, Marquise de Prie
Attributed to Louis Michel van Loo
Musée du Louvre Service d'étude
et de documentation du département des Peintures

BUNDESKANZLERAMT ▌ KUNST

Set in 10.5 on 13.5 Monotype Baskerville
and printed in Britain
on Shakespeare Laid paper

TWILIGHT

MADAME DE PRIE returning from her morning drive on the day when the King dismissed her lover the Duke of Bourbon from his position as prime-minister in charge of the affairs of state, thought, as the two footman at the door bowed low to her, that she caught them suppressing a smile at the same time, which vexed her. She did not let it show for the moment, and walked past them and up the steps with composure. But when she reached the first landing on the stairs she abruptly turned her head back, and she saw a broad grin on the lips of the garrulous pair, although it rapidly disappeared as they bowed again in alarm.

Now she knew enough. And up in her salon, where an officer of the royal bodyguard with much gold braid about his person was waiting for her with a letter, she appeared to be in as serene and almost exuberant a mood as if this were merely a conventional call on a friend. Although she noticed the royal seal on the letter and the rather awkward manner of the officer who was aware of the embarrassing nature of his message, she showed neither curiosity nor concern. Without opening the letter or even examining it more closely she made light conversation with the aristocratic young soldier, and on recognising him as a Breton by his accent told him the story of a lady who could never stand Bretons, because one of his countrymen had once become her lover against her will. She was in high spirits and made risqué jokes, partly from a deliberate intention of showing how carefree she was, partly from habit, for in general a careless and easy levity made all her dissimulations seem natural, even transforming them into sincerity. She talked until she really forgot the royal letter, which she creased as she held it in her hands. But finally, after all, she broke the seal.

The letter contained the royal order, expressed briefly and with remarkably little civility, for her to leave court at once and retire to her estate of Courbépine in Normandy. She had fallen into disfavour, her enemies had won at last; even before the King's message arrived she had known it from the smiles of her footmen at the door. But she did not give herself away. The officer carefully observed her eyes as they ran along the lines. They did not flicker, and now that she turned to him again a smile sparkled in them. "His Majesty is very anxious about my health, and would like me to leave the heat of the city and retire to my château. Tell his Majesty that I will comply with his wishes immediately." She smiled as she spoke, as if there were some secret meaning in her words. The officer raised his hat to her and left, with a bow.

But the door had hardly closed behind him before the

smile fell from her lips like a withered leaf. She angrily crumpled up the letter. How many such missives, each sealing a human fate, had been sent out into the world under the royal name when she herself had dictated their contents! And now, after she had ruled all France for two years, her enemies dared to banish her from court with a sheet of paper like this! She hadn't expected so much courage from them. To be sure, the young King had never liked her and was ill-disposed towards her, but had she made Marie Leszczynska Queen of France only to be exiled now, just because a mob had rioted outside her windows and there was some kind of famine in the country? For a moment she wondered whether to resist the King's command: the Regent of France, the Duke of Orléans, had been her lover, and anyone who now held power and a high position at court owed it all to her. She did not lack for friends. But she was too proud to appear as a beggar where she was known as a mistress; no one in France was ever to see her with anything but a smiling face. Her exile couldn't last more than a few days, until tempers had calmed down, and then her friends would make sure she was recalled. In her mind, she was already looking forward to her revenge, and soothed her anger with that idea.

Madame de Prie went about her departure with the utmost secrecy. She gave no one a chance to feel sorry for her and received no callers, to avoid having to tell them she was going away. She wanted to disappear suddenly, in mysterious and dashing style, leaving a riddle calculated to confuse the whole court permanently linked to her absence, for it was a peculiarity of her character that she always wished to deceive, to veil whatever she was really doing with a lie. The only person she herself visited was the Count of Belle-Isle, her mortal enemy and the man behind her banishment. She sought him out to show him her smile, her unconcern, her self-confidence. She told him how she welcomed the opportunity of a rest from the stress of life at court, she told blatant lies that clearly showed him the depth of her hatred and contempt. The Count only smiled coldly and said he thought that she would find it hard to bear so long a period of solitude, and he gave the word "long" a strange emphasis that alarmed her. But she controlled herself, and civilly invited him to come and hunt on her estate.

In the afternoon she did meet one of her lovers in her little house in the rue Apolline, and told him to keep her well informed about everything that went on at court. She left that evening. She did not want to drive through the city in her open chaise during the day, because the common people had been hostile to her since the riot that cost human lives, and in addition she was determined to keep her disappearance a mystery. She intended to leave by night and return by day. She left her house just as it was, as if she were going away for only a day or so, and at the moment when the carriage began to move off she said out loud—knowing that her words would find their way back to court—that she was taking a short journey for the sake of her health and would soon be back. And she had schooled herself to wear the mask of dissimulation so well that, genuinely reassured by her own lie, she soon fell into an easy sleep in the jolting carriage, and woke only when she was well outside Paris and past the first posting station, surprised to find herself in a carriage at all, bound for something new, not knowing yet whether it would be good or bad. She felt only that the wheels were turning under her and she had no control over them, that she was gliding into the unknown, but she could not feel any serious anxiety, and soon fell asleep again.

The journey to Normandy was long and tedious, but her first day in Courbépine restored her cheerfulness. Her restless, fanciful mind, always lusting after novelty, discovered an unaccustomed charm in giving itself up to the crystalline purity of a summer's day in the country. She lost herself in a thousand follies, amused herself by walking down the avenues of the park, jumping hedges and trying to catch fluttering butterflies, clad in a dress white as blossom with pale ribbons in her hair, like the little girl she had once been and whom she had thought long dead in her. She walked and walked, and for the first time in years felt the pleasure of letting her limbs relax in the rhythm of her pace, just as she delightedly rediscovered everything about the simple life that she had forgotten in her days at court. She lay in the emerald grass and looked up at the clouds. How strange it was: she hadn't looked at a cloud for years, and she wondered whether clouds were as beautifully outlined, as fluffily white, as pure and airy above the buildings of Paris. For the first time she saw the sky as something real, and its blue vault, sprinkled with white, reminded her of the wonderful Chinese vase that a German prince had recently given her as a present, except that the sky was even lovelier, bluer, more rounded, and full of mild, fragrant air that felt as soft as silk. After hurrying from one entertainment to the next in Paris, she delighted in doing nothing, and the silence around her was as delicious as a cool drink. She now realised, for the first time, that she felt nothing for all the people who had flocked around her at Versailles, she neither loved nor hated any of them, she felt no more for them than for the peasants standing there on the outskirts of the wood with their large, flashing scythes, sometimes shading their eyes with a hand to peer curiously at her. She became more and more exuberant; she played with the young trees, jumped in the air until she could catch the hanging branches, let them spring up again, and laughed out loud when a few white blossoms, as if struck by an arrow, fell into the hand she held out to catch them or the hair she was wearing loose for the first time in years. With the wonderful facility of forgetfulness available to women of no great depth throughout their lives, she did not remember that she was in exile and before that had ruled France, playing with the fate of others as casually as she played now with butterflies and glimmering trees. She cast aside five, ten, fifteen years of her life and was Mademoiselle Pleuneuf again, daughter of the Geneva banker, playing in the convent garden, a small, thin, high-spirited girl of fifteen who knew nothing of Paris and the wide world.

In the afternoon she helped the maids with the harvest: she thought it uncommonly amusing to bind up the big sheaves and fling them exuberantly up to the farm cart. And she sat among them—they had been awestruck at first and behaved shyly—on top of the fully loaded wagon, dangling her legs, laughing with the young fellows and then, when the dancing began, whirling around with the best. It all felt to her like a successful masquerade at court, and she looked forward to telling everyone in Paris how charmingly she had spent her time, dancing with wild flowers in her hair and drinking from the same pitcher as the peasants. She noticed the reality of these things as little as she had felt, at Versailles, that the games of shepherds and shepherdesses were only pretence. Her heart was lost to the pleasure of the moment, it lied in telling the truth and was honest even while it intended to deceive, for she only ever knew what she felt. And what she felt now was delight and rapture running through her veins. The idea that she was out of favour was laughable.

But next morning a dark vestige of ill humour seeped in, mingling with the crystalline merriment of her hours. Waking itself was painful; she tumbled from the black night of dreamless sleep into day as if from warm, sultry air into icy water. She didn't know what had woken her. It was not the light, for a dull, rainy day was dawning outside the tear-stained windows. And it was not the noise either, for there were no voices here, only the fixed, piercing eyes of the dead looking down at her from their pictures on the wall. She was awake and didn't know why or what for; nothing appealed to her here or tempted her.

And she thought how different waking up in Paris had been. She had danced and talked all evening, had spent half the night with her friends, and then came the wonderful sleep of exhaustion, with bright images still flickering on in her excited mind. And in the morning, with her eyes closed and as if still in a dream, she heard muted voices in the anterooms, and no sooner did her *levée* begin than they came streaming in: the royal dukes of France, petitioners, lovers, friends, all vying for her favour and bringing the suitor's gift of solicitous cheerfulness. Everyone had a story to tell, laughed, chattered, all the latest news and gossip came to her bedside, and her moment of waking carried her straight from those bright dreams into the full tide of life. The smile she had worn on her sleeping lips did not vanish but remained at the corners of her mouth, hovering there in high spirits like a bird swinging in its cage.

The day led her on from these images of her friends to those friends themselves, and they stayed with her as she dressed, as she drove out, as she ate, until far into the night again. She felt herself constantly carried on by this murmuring torrent, restless as the waves, dancing in never-ending rhythm and rocking the flowery boat of her life.

Here, however, the torrent cast her moment of awakening up on a rock, where it lay stranded on the beach of the hours, immobile and useless. Nothing tempted her to get up. Yesterday's innocent amusements had lost their charm; her curiosity, used to being indulged, was of the kind that quickly wore off. Her room was empty, as if airless, and she felt empty too in this solitude where no one asked for her: empty, useless, washed out and drained; she had to remind herself slowly why and how she had come to be here. What did she expect of the day that made her stare so hard at the clock, as it paced indefatigably through the silence with its gentle, tremulous gait?

At last she remembered. She had asked the Prince of Alincourt, the only one of her former lovers for whom she felt any real affection, to send her news from court daily by a mounted messenger. All yesterday she had forgotten what a sensation her disappearance must have been in Paris; now she longed to enjoy that triumph. And the messenger soon arrived, but not the message. Alincourt wrote her a few indifferent banalities, news of the King's health, visits from foreign princes, and let the letter peter out in friendly wishes for her well-being. Not a word about herself and her disappearance. She was angry. Hadn't the news been made public? Or had no one really believed her pretence that she was coming to this tedious place for the sake of her health?

The messenger, a simple, bull-necked groom, shrugged his shoulders. He knew nothing. She concealed her annoyance and wrote back to Alincourt—without showing her displeasure—to thank him for his news and urge him to continue writing to her, telling her everything, all the details. She hoped not to stay in the country long, she said, although she liked it here very well. She didn't even notice that she was lying to him.

But then the rest of the day was so long. The hours here, like the people themselves, seemed to go at a more sedate pace, and she knew no means of making them pass any faster. She didn't know what to do with herself: everything in her was mute, all the brilliant music of her heart dead as a musical clock when the key has been lost. She tried all kinds of things, she sent for books, but even the wittiest of them seemed to her mere printed pages. Disquiet came over her, she missed all the people among whom she had lived for years. She sent the servants hither and thither to no good purpose with imperious commands: she wanted to hear footsteps on the stairs, to see people, to create an illusion of the busy hum of messages, to deceive herself, but like all her plans at present, it didn't work. Eating disgusted her, like the room and the sky and her servants: all she wanted now was night and deep, black, dreamless sleep until morning, when a more satisfactory message would arrive.

At last evening came, but it was dismal here! Nothing but the coming of darkness, the disappearance of everything, the extinction of the light. Evening here was an end, whereas in Paris it had been the beginning of all pleasures. Here it let the night pour in, there it lit gilded candles in the royal halls, made the air sparkle in your eyes, kindled, warmed, intoxicated and inspired the heart. Here it only made you more anxious. She wandered from room to room: silence lurked in all of them, like a savage animal sated with all the years when no one had been here, and she feared it might leap on her. The floorboards groaned, the books creaked in their bindings as soon as you touched them; something in the spinet moaned in fright like a beaten child when she touched the keys and summoned up a tearful sound. Everything joined in the darkness to resist her, the intruder.

Then, shivering, she had lights lit all over the house. She tried to stay in one room, but she was constantly impelled to move on, she fled from room to room as if that would calm her. But everywhere she came up against the invisible wall of the silence that had ruled this place by right for years, and would not be dismissed. Even the lights seemed to feel it; they hissed quietly and wept hot drops of wax.

Seen from outside, however, the château shone brightly with its thirty sparkling windows, as if there were great festivities here. Groups of villagers stood outside, amazed and wondering aloud where so many people had suddenly come from. But the figure that they saw flitting like a shadow past first one window and then another was always the same: madame de Prie, pacing desperately up and down like a wild beast in the prison of her inner solitude, looking through the window for something that never came.

On the third day she lost control of her impatience and it turned violent. The solitude oppressed her; she needed people, or at least news of people, of the court, the natural home of her whole being with all its ramifications, of her friends, something to excite or merely touch her. She couldn't wait for the messenger, and early in the morning she rode for three hours to meet him. It was raining, and there was a high wind; her hair, heavy with water, pulled her head back, and the wind blew rain in her face so hard that she saw nothing. Her freezing hands could hardly hold the reins. Finally she galloped back, had her wet clothes stripped off, and took refuge in bed again. She waited feverishly, clenching her teeth on the covers. Now she understood the Count of Belle-Isle's menacing smile as he said that she would find so long a period of solitude hard to bear. And it had been only three days!

At last the courier came. She did not pretend any longer, but avidly tore the seal off the letter with her nails, like a starving man tearing the husk off a fruit. There was a great deal about the court in it: her eye ran down the lines in search of her name. Nothing, nothing. But one name did stand out like fire: her position as lady in waiting had been given to madame de Calaincourt.

For a moment she trembled and felt quite weak. So it was not a case of fleeting disfavour but permanent exile: it was her death sentence, and she loved life. She leaped suddenly out of bed, feeling no shame in front of the courier, and half-naked, shaking with the cold, she wrote letter after letter with a wild craving. She abandoned her show of pride. She wrote to the King, although she knew he hated her; she promised in the humblest, most pitifully grovelling of terms never to try meddling in affairs of state again. She wrote to Maria Leszczynska, reminding her that she was Queen of France only through the agency of madame de Prie;

she wrote to the ministers, promising them money; she turned to her friends. She urged Voltaire, whom she had saved from the Bastille, to write an elegy on her departure from court and to read it aloud. She ordered her secretary to commission lampoons on her enemies and have them distributed in pamphlet form. She wrote twenty such letters with her fevered hand, all begging for just one thing: Paris, the world, salvation from this solitude. They were no longer letters but screams. Then she opened a casket, gave the courier a handful of gold pieces, told him that even if he rode his horse to death he must be in Paris tonight. Only here had she learned what an hour really meant. Startled, he was going to thank her, but she drove him out.

Then she sought shelter in bed again. She was freezing. A harsh cough shook her thin frame. She lay staring ahead, always waiting for the clock on the mantelpiece to reach the hour and strike at last. But the hours were stubborn, they were not to be hounded with curses, with pleas, with gold, they went sleepily around. The servants came, she sent them all out, she would show no one her despair, she did not want food, or words, she wanted nothing from anyone. The rain fell incessantly outside, and she was as chilly as if she were standing out there shivering like the shrubs with their arms helplessly outstretched. One question went up and down in her mind like the swing of a pendulum: why, why, why,

why? Why had God done this to her? Had she sinned so much?

She tugged at the bell-pull and told them to fetch the local priest. It soothed her to think that someone lived here to whom she could talk and confide her fears.

The priest did not delay, more particularly as he had been told that madame was ill. She could not help smiling when he came in, thinking of her abbé in Paris with his fine and delicate hands, the bright glance that rested on her almost tenderly, his courtly conversation which made you quite forget that he was taking confession. The abbé of Courbépine was portly and broad-shouldered, and his boots creaked as he trudged through the doorway. Everything about him was red: his plump hands, his face, weathered by the wind, his big ears, but there was something friendly about him as he offered her his great paw in greeting and sat down in an armchair. The horror in the room seemed to fear his weighty presence and cringed in a corner: filled by his loud voice the room appeared warmer, livelier, and it seemed to madame de Prie that she breathed more easily now that he was here. He did not know exactly why he had been summoned, and made clumsy conversation, spoke of his parish work, and Paris which he knew only by hearsay, he demonstrated his scholarship, spoke of Descartes and the dangerous works of the sieur de Montaigne. She put in a word here and there, abstractedly; her thoughts were buzzing like a swarm of flies, she just wanted to listen, to hear a human voice, to raise it like a dam holding back the sea of loneliness that threatened to drown her. When, afraid he was disturbing her he was about to stop talking, she encouraged him with ardent kindness which was really nothing but fear. She promised to call on the reverend gentleman, invited him to visit her often; the seductive side of her nature, which had cast such a spell in Paris, emerged extravagantly from her dreamy silence. And the abbé stayed until it was dark.

But as soon as he left she felt as if the weight of the silence were descending on her twice as heavily as before, as if she alone had to hold up the high ceiling, she alone must keep back the advancing darkness. She had never known how much a single human being can mean to another, because she had never been lonely before. She had never thought more of other people than of air, and one does not feel the air, but now that solitude was choking her, only now did she realise how much she needed them, recognising how much they meant to her even when they deceived and told lies, how she herself drew everything from their presence, their easy manners, their confidence and cheerfulness. She had been immersed for decades in the tide of society, never knowing that it nourished and bore her up, but now, stranded like a fish on the beach of solitude, she flinched in despair and convulsive pain. She was freezing and feverishly hot at once. She felt her own body, was startled to find how cold it was; all its sensuous warmth seemed to have died away, her blood surged sluggishly through her veins like gelatine, she felt as if she were lying here in the silence inside the coffin of her own corpse. And suddenly a hot sob of despair tore through her. Alarmed at first, she tried to suppress it, but there was no one here, here she did not have to dissimulate, she was alone with herself for the first time. And she willingly abandoned herself to the sweet pain of feeling hot tears run down her icy cheeks, while she heard her own sobbing in the terrible silence.

She made haste to return the abbé's visit. The house was deserted, no letters came—she herself knew that no one in Paris had much time for petitioners, and she had to do something, anything, even if it was just playing backgammon, or talking, or simply finding out how someone else talked. Somehow she must defy the tedium advancing ever more menacingly and murderously on her heart. She hurried through the village; she felt nauseated by everything that partook in any way of the name of Courbépine and reminded her of her exile. The abbé's little house lay at the end of the village street, surrounded by green countryside. It was not much higher than a barn, but flowers framed the tiny windows and their tangled foliage hung down over the door, so that she had to bend down to avoid being caught in their fragrant toils.

The abbé was not alone. With him at his desk sat a young man whom, in great confusion at the honour of such a visit, he introduced as his nephew. The abbé was preparing him for his studies, although he was not to be a priest—a vocation for which so much must be given up! This was meant as a gallant jest. Madame de Prie smiled, not so much at the rather clumsy compliment as at the amusing embarrassment of the young man, who blushed red and didn't know where to look. He was a tall country fellow with a bony, red-cheeked face, yellow hair and a rather artless expression: he seemed clumsy and brutish with his awkward limbs, but at the moment his extreme respect for her kept his boorishness within bounds and made him look childishly helpless. He scarcely dared to answer her questions, stuttered and stammered, put his hands in his pockets, took them out again, and madame de Prie, enchanted by his embarrassment, asked him question after question—it did her good to find someone who was confused and small in her presence again, who felt that he was a supplicant, subservient to her. The abbé spoke for him, praised his passion for the noble vocation of scholarship, his other good qualities, and told her it was the boy's great wish to be able to complete his studies at the university in Paris. He himself, to be sure, was poor and could not help his nephew much, the boy also lacked the patronage that alone smoothed the path to high office, and he pressingly recommended him to her favour. He knew that she was all-powerful at court; a single word would suffice to make the young student's boldest dreams come true.

Madame de Prie smiled bitterly into the darkness: so she was supposed to be all-powerful at court, and couldn't even compel anyone to answer a single letter or grant a single request. Yet it was good to feel that no one here knew of her helplessness and her fall from grace. Even the semblance of power warmed her heart now. She controlled herself: yes, she would certainly recommend the young man, who from what so estimable an advocate as the abbé said of him must surely be worthy of every favour. She asked him to come and talk to her tomorrow so that she could assess his qualities. She would recommend him at court, she said, she would give him a letter of introduction to her friend the Queen and the members of the Academy (reminding herself, as she said so, that not one of them had sent a single line in reply to her letters).

The old abbé was quivering with delight, and tears ran down his fat cheeks. He kissed her hands, wandered around the room as if drunk, while the young fellow stood there with a dazed expression, unable to utter a word. When madame de Prie decided to leave he did not budge, but stayed rooted to the spot, until the abbé surreptitiously indicated, with a vigorous gesture, that he should escort his benefactress back to the château. He walked beside her, stammering out thanks, and tangling his words up whenever she looked at him. It made her feel quite cheerful. For the first time she felt the old relish, mingled with slight contempt, of seeing a human being powerless before her. It revived the desire to toy with others which had become a necessity of life to her during her years of power. He stopped at the gateway of the château, bowed clumsily and strode away with his stiff, rustic gait, hardly giving her time to remind him to come and see her tomorrow.

She watched him go, smiling to herself. He was clumsy and naïve, but all the same he was alive and passionate, not dead like everything else around her. He was fire, and she was freezing. Her body was starved here too, accustomed as it was to caresses and embraces; her eyes, if they were to have any lively brilliance, must reflect the sparkling desires of the young that came her way daily in Paris. She watched for a long time as he walked away: this could be a toy, admittedly made of hard wood, rough-hewn and artless, but still a toy to help her pass the time.

Next morning the young man called. Madame de Prie, who weary as she was with inactivity and discontent did not usually rise until late in the afternoon, decided to receive the caller in her bed. First she had herself carefully adorned by her lady's maid, with a little red colour on her lips, which were getting paler and paler. Then she told the maid to admit her visitor.

The door slowly creaked open. Hesitantly and very awkwardly, the young man made his way in. He had put on his best garments, which none the less were the Sunday clothes of a rustic, and smelled rather too strongly of various greasy ointments. His gaze wandered searchingly from the floor to the ceiling of the darkened room, and he seemed relieved to find no one there, until an encouraging greeting came from beneath the pink cloud of the canopy over the bed. He started, for he either did not know or had forgotten that great ladies in Paris received visitors at their *levée*. He made some kind of backwards movement, as if he had stepped into deep water, and his cheeks flushed a deep red, betraying embarrassment which she enjoyed to the full and which charmed her. In honeyed tones, she invited him to come closer. It amused her to treat him with the utmost civility.

He carefully approached, as if walking a narrow plank with great depths of foaming water to right and left of him. And she held out her small, slim hand, which he cautiously took in his sturdy fingers as if he were afraid of breaking it, raising it reverently to his lips. With a friendly gesture, she invited him to sit in a comfortable armchair beside her bed, and he dropped into it as if his knees had suddenly been broken.

He felt a little safer sitting there. Now the whole room couldn't go on circling wildly around him, the floor couldn't rock like waves. However, the unusual sight still confused him, the loose silk of the covers seemed to mould the shape of her naked body, and the pink cloud of the canopy hovered like mist. He dared not look, yet he felt that he couldn't keep his eyes fixed on the floor for ever. His hands, his useless large, red hands, moved up and down the arms of the chair as if he had to hold on tight. Then they took fright at their own restlessness, and lay in his lap, frozen like heavy clods. There was a burning, almost tearful sensation in his eyes, fear tore at all his muscles, and his throat felt powerless to utter a word.

She was delighted by his awkwardness. It pleased her to let the silence drag mercilessly on, to watch, smiling, as he struggled to utter his first word, repeatedly unable to bring out anything but a stammer. She liked to see a young man as strong as an ox trembling and looking helplessly around him. Finally she took pity on him, and began asking him about his intentions, in which she contrived to pretend an uncommon amount of interest, so that he gradually plucked up his courage again. He talked about his studies, the church fathers and philosophers, and she chatted to him without knowing much about it. And when the self-important sobriety with which he put forward his opinions and expanded on them began to bore her, she amused herself by making little movements to discompose him. Sometimes she plucked at the bedspread as if it were about to slide off; at an abrupt gesture from the speaker she suddenly raised a bare arm from the crumpled silk; she wriggled her feet under the covers; and every time she did this he stopped, became confused, stumbled over his words or brought them out tumbling over each other, his face assumed an increasingly tortured and tense expression, and now and then she saw a vein run swift as a snake across his forehead. The game entertained her. She liked his boyish confusion a thousand times better than his well-turned rhetoric. And now she sought to discomfit him verbally too.

"You mustn't keep thinking so much of your studies and your sterling qualities! There are certain skills that matter more in Paris. You must learn to put yourself forward. You're an attractive man; be clever, make good use of your youth, above all, don't neglect women. Women mean everything in Paris, so our weakness must be your strength. Learn to choose your lovers and exploit them well, and you'll become a minister. Have you ever had a lover here?"

The young man started. All of sudden his face was dark as blood. An overpowering sense of intolerable strain urged him to run to the door, but there was a heaviness in him, as if he were dazed by the fragrance of this woman's perfume, by her breath. All his muscles felt cramped, his chest was tense, he felt himself running crazily wild.

Then there was a crack. His clutching fingers had broken the arm of the chair. He jumped up in alarm, unspeakably humiliated by this mishap, but she, charmed by his elemental passion, just smiled and said, "Oh, you mustn't take fright like that when you're asked a question that you're not used to. You'll find it often happens in Paris. But you must learn a few more courtly manners, and I'll help you. I find it difficult to do without my secretary anyway; I would like it if you'd take his place here."

His eyes shining, he stammered effusive thanks and pressed her hand so hard that it hurt. She smiled, a sad smile—here it was again, the old delusion of imagining herself loved, when the reality was that one man had a position in mind, another his vanity, a third his career. All the same, it was so delightful to keep forgetting that. And here she had no one to delude but herself. Three days later he was her lover.

But the dangerous boredom had only been scared away, not mortally wounded. It dragged itself through the empty rooms again, lying in wait behind their doors. Only unwelcome news came from Paris. The King did not reply to her at all; Marie Leszczynska sent a few

frosty lines inquiring after her health and carefully
avoiding any hint of friendly feeling. She thought the
lampoons were tasteless and offensive, besides showing
too clearly who had commissioned them, which was
enough to make her position at court even at worse, in
so far as anyone there still remembered her. Nor was
there a word in the letter she received from her friend
Alincourt about any return, not even a glimmer of
hope. She felt like a woman who was thought dead but
wakes in her coffin underground, screaming and raving
and hammering on its sides, while no one hears her up
above, men and women walk lightly over the ground,
and her voice chokes alone in the solitude. Madame de
Prie wrote a few more letters, but with the same feeling
that she was buried alive and screaming, well aware
that no one would hear her, that she was hammering
helplessly against the walls of her isolation. However,
writing them passed the time, and here in Courbépine
time was her bitterest enemy.

Her game with the young man soon bored her too. She
had never shown any constancy in her affections (it was
the main reason behind her fall from favour), and this
young fellow's few words of love, the awkwardness that
he soon forgot once she had given him good clothes, silk
stockings and fine buckles for his shoes, could not keep
her mind occupied. Her nature was so sated with the
company of crowds that she soon wearied of a single

man, and as soon as she was alone she seemed to herself repulsive and wretched. Seducing this timid peasant, schooling his clumsy caresses, making the bear dance had been a pretty game; she found possessing him was tedious, indeed positively embarrassing.

And furthermore, he no longer pleased her. She had been charmed by the adoration he had shown her, his devotion, his confusion. But he soon shed those qualities and developed a familiarity that repelled her; his once humble gaze was now full of relish and self-satisfaction. He preened in his fine clothes, and she suspected that he showed off to the village in them. A kind of hatred gradually arose in her, because he had gained all this from her unhappiness and loneliness, because he was healthy and ate with a hearty appetite, while she ate less and less out of rage and her injured feelings, and grew thin and weak. He took her for granted as his lover, oaf that he was, he lolled contentedly in the idle bed of his conquest, instead of showing his first amazement when she gave him the gift of herself, he grew apathetic and lazy, and she, bitterly envious, burning with unhappiness and ignominy, hated his repellent satisfaction, his boorish avarice and base pride. And she hated herself for sinking so low that she must reach out to such crude folk if she was not to founder in the mud of solitude.

She began to provoke and torment him. She had never really been vicious, but she felt a need to avenge herself on someone for everything, for her enemies' triumph, her exile from Paris, her unanswered letters, for Courbépine. And she had no one else to hand. She wanted to rouse him from his lethargic ease, make him feel small again, not so happy, make him cringe. She mercilessly reproached him for his red hands, his lack of sophistication, his bad manners, but he, with a man's healthy instinct, took little notice now of the woman who had once summoned him to her. He was defiant, he laughed, and indignantly shook off her sarcasm. But she did not stop: irritating someone made a nice game to relieve her boredom. She tried to make him jealous, told him on every occasion about her lovers in Paris, counted them on her fingers for him. She showed him presents she had been given, she exaggerated and told lies. But he merely felt flattered to think that, after all those dukes and princes, she had chosen him. He smacked his lips with satisfaction and was not discomposed. That enraged her even more. She told him other, worse things, she lied to him about the grooms and valets she had had. His brow darkened at last. She saw it, laughed, and went on. Suddenly he struck the table with his fist.

"That's enough! Why are you telling me all this?"

Her expression was perfectly innocent. "Because I like to."

"But I don't want to hear it."

"I do, my dear, or I wouldn't do it."

He said nothing, but bit his lip. She had so naturally commanding a tone of voice that he felt like a servant. He clenched his fists. How like an animal he is when he's angry, she thought, feeling both revulsion and fear. She sensed the danger in the atmosphere. But there was too much anger pent up in her, she couldn't stop tormenting him. She began again.

"What strange ideas you have of life, my dear. Do you think Parisians live as you do in your hovels here, where one is slowly bored to death?"

His nostrils flared; he snorted. Then he said, "People don't have to come here if they think it's so boring."

She felt the pang deep within her. So he knew about her exile too. She supposed the valet had spread the news. She felt weaker now that he knew, and smiled to veil her fear.

"My dear, there are reasons that you may not necessarily understand even if you've learned a little Latin. Perhaps you would have found it more useful to study better manners."

He said nothing, but she heard him snorting quietly with rage. That aroused her even more and she felt something like a sensual desire to hurt him.

"And there you stand proud as a cockerel on the dung-hill. Why do you snort like that? You're acting like a lout!"

"We can't all be princes or dukes or grooms."

He was red in the face and had clenched his fists. She, however, poisoned by unhappiness, leaped to her feet.

"Be quiet! You forget who I am. I won't be spoken to like that by a rustic oaf!"

He made a gesture.

"Be quiet! Or else … "

"Or else?"

He impudently faced her. And it occurred to her that she had no 'or else' left. She couldn't have anyone sent to the Bastille, or reduced to the ranks or dismissed, she couldn't command or forbid anyone to do or not to do something. She was nothing, only a defenceless woman like hundreds of thousands in France, vulnerable to any insult, any injustice.

"Or else," she said, fighting for breath, "I'll have you thrown out by the servants."

He shrugged his shoulders and turned. He was going to leave.

But she wouldn't let him. He was not to be the one to throw her over! Another man rejecting her—least of all must it be this one. All her anger suddenly broke out, the accumulated bitterness of days, and she went for him as if she were drunk.

"Get out! Do you think I need you, you fool of a peasant, just because I felt sorry for you? Go away! Don't soil my floors any more. Go where you like but not to Paris, and not to me. Get out! I hate you, your avarice, your simplicity, your stupid satisfaction—you disgust me. Get out!"

Then the unexpected happened. As she so suddenly flung her hatred at him, he had been holding his fists clenched in front of him like an invisible shield, but now they suddenly came down on her with the impact of falling stones. She screamed and stared at him. But he struck and struck in blind, vengeful rage, intoxicated by the awareness of his strength, he struck her, taking out on her all a peasant's envy of the distinguished and clever aristocrat, all the hatred of a man despised for a woman, he hammered it all into her weak, flinching, convulsed body. She screamed at first, then whimpered quietly and fell silent. The humiliation hurt her more than the blows. She fell silent, felt his rage, and still preserved her silence.

Then he stopped, exhausted, and horrified by what he had done. A shudder ran through her body. He thought she was about to stand up, and he fled, afraid of her glance. But it was only the weeping that she had held back suddenly tearing convulsively through her body.

And so she broke her last toy herself.

The door had closed behind him long ago, and still she did not move. She lay there like an animal hunted to death, breathing quietly but stertorously, and quite without fear, without feelings, without any sense of pain or

38

shame. She was full of an unspeakable weariness, she felt no wish for revenge, no indignation, just weariness, an unspeakable weariness as if all her blood had flowed out of her together with her tears and only her lifeless body lay here, held down by its own weight. She did not try to stand up, she didn't know what to do with herself after such an experience.

The evening slowly entered the room, and she did not feel it. For evening comes quietly. It does not look boldly through the window like mid-day, it seeps from the walls like dark water, raises the ceiling into a void, brings everything gently floating down into its soundless torrent. When she looked up, there was darkness around her and silence, except for the sound of the little clock mincing along into infinity somewhere. The curtains fell in dark folds as if some fearful monster were hiding behind them, the doors seemed to have sunk into the wall in some way, making the room look sealed and black around her, like a nailed-up coffin. There was no way in or out any more, it was all boundless yet barred, everything seemed to weigh down, compressing the air so that she could gasp, not breathe.

At the far end of the room shone a path into the unknown: the tall mirror there gleamed faintly in the dark like the nocturnal surface of a marshy pool, and now, as she rose, something white swirled out of it. She got to her feet, went closer, it surged from the mirror like smoke, a ghostly creature: she herself, coming closer and quickly withdrawing again.

She felt dread. Something in her cried out for light, but she did not want to call anyone. She struck the tinder herself, and then one by one lit the candles in the dully glowing bronze candelabrum standing on its marble console. The flames flickered, quivering as they felt their way into the dark, like someone overheated stepping into a cool bath; they retreated, came forward again, and at last a trembling, circular cloud of light rose above the candelabrum and hovered there, casting more and more circles of light on the ceiling. High above, where delicate *amoretti* with wings of cloud usually rocked in the blue sky, grey, misty shadows now lay, with the soft lightning of the quivering candle-flames flashing fitfully through them. The objects all around seemed to have been roused from sleep; they stood there motionless, with shadows creeping high behind them as if animals had been crouching there, giving them a fearful look.

However, the mirror enticed and allured her. Something was always moving in it when she looked. Otherwise, all around her was silent and hostile, the objects were sleepy, human beings rejected her. She could ask no questions, couldn't complain to anyone, but there was something in the mirror that gave an answer, did not remain indifferent, moved and looked significantly at her. But what should she ask it? She had seldom asked if she was beautiful in Paris. The bright eyes of the men who desired her had been her mirror. She knew she was beautiful from her triumphs, her passionate nights, from the amazement of the common people when she drove to Versailles in her carriage. She had believed them even when they lied, for confidence in her own power was the secret of her strength. But now, what was she now that she had been humbled?

She looked anxiously into the flickering light in the glass, as if her fate stood in the mirror looking back at her. She started in alarm: was that really herself? Her cheeks looked hollow and dull, a bitter set to her mouth mocked her, her eyes lay deep in their sockets and looked out in fear as if searching for help. She shook herself. This was just a nightmare. And she smiled at the mirror. But the smile was returned frostily, scornfully. She felt her body: no, the mirror did not lie, she had grown thin, thin as a child, and the rings hung loose on her fingers. She felt the blood flow more coldly in her veins. She was full of dread. Was everything over, youth as well? A furious desire came over her to mock herself, celebrated as she was, the mistress of France, and as if in a dream she spoke the lines that Voltaire had written when dedicating his play to her, the lines that her flatterers liked to repeat:

Vous qui possedez la beauté
Sans être vaine et coquette

Et l'extrême vivacité
Sans être jamais indiscrète,
Vous à qui donnèrent les Dieux
Tant des lumières naturelles
Un esprit juste, gracieux,
Solide dans le sérieux
Et charmant dans les bagatelles. *

Every word now seemed to express derision, and she stared and stared into the mirror to see if the woman there was not mocking her too.

She raised the candelabrum to get a better view of herself. And the closer she held it the more she seemed to age. Every minute she spent looking into the mirror seemed to put years on her life, she saw herself grow paler and paler, becoming more wan, sicklier, older all the time, she felt herself aging, her whole life seemed to be passing away. She trembled. She saw her fate horribly revealed in the mirror, the entire story of her decline, and she couldn't take her eyes off it, but stared and stared at the white, distorted mask of the old woman who was herself.

Then, suddenly, the candles all flickered at once as if in alarm, the flames turned blue and tried to fly up from

---

* Lady, yours is a beauty bright, never flirtatious, never vain; your liveliness will show no spite, and never seeks to inflict pain. Was all the bounty of the mind, a spirit gracious, full of love. In graver questions wise you prove, in matters light, charming and kind.

their wicks. A dark figure stood in the mirror, its hand reaching out to her.

She uttered a piercing scream, and in self-defence flung the bronze candelabrum at the mirror. A thousand sparks sprang from the glass. The candles fell to the floor and went out. There was darkness around her and in her as she collapsed unconscious. She had seen her fate.

The courier who had entered the room with news from Paris, and whose sudden appearance in the mirror-frame had so alarmed madame de Prie, saw only the shimmering of the broken shards of glass, and heard the sound of a fall in the darkness. He ran to fetch the servants. They found madame de Prie lying motionless on the floor among the sparkling glass splinters and the extinguished candles, her eyes closed. Only her bluish lips trembled slightly, showing a sign of life. They carried her to her bed, and a servant set out to ride to Amfreville and fetch the doctor.

But the sick woman soon came round, and with difficulty brought herself back to reality amidst the frightened faces. She did not know exactly how she had come here, but she controlled her fear and weariness in front of the others, kept her ever-ready smile on her bloodless lips although her face had now frozen to a mask, and asked in a voice that endeavoured to be carefree, even cheerful, what had happened to her. In alarm, and evasively, the servants told her. She did not reply, but smiled and reached for the letter.

However, it was difficult for her to keep that smile on her face. Her friend wrote to say that he had succeeded in speaking to the King at last. The King was still extremely angry with her, because she had wrecked the country's finances and roused the people against her, but there was some hope of having her recalled to Paris in two or three years' time. The letter shook in her hands. Was she to live away from Paris for two years without people around her, without power? She was not strong enough to bear such solitude. It was her death sentence. She knew that she couldn't breathe without happiness, without power, without youth, without love; after ruling France, she couldn't live here like a peasant woman.

And all of a sudden she understood the figure in the mirror that had reached out for her, and the extinguishing of the flames: she must put an end to it before she grew really old, wholly ugly and wholly unhappy. She refused to see the doctor, who had now arrived; only the King could have helped her. And as he would not, she must help herself. The thought no longer hurt her. She had died long ago, on the day when the officer stood in her room and took everything from her that kept her alive: the air of Paris, the only place where she could breathe; the power that was her plaything; the admiration and triumph to which she owed her strength. The woman who roamed these empty rooms, lonely, bored, and humiliated, was no longer madame de Prie, was an aging, unhappy, ugly creature whom she must kill so that it would not dishonour the name that had once shone brightly over France.

Now that the exiled woman had decided to put an end to it herself, her sense of frozen heaviness, her urgent disquiet had left her. She had a purpose again, an occupation, something that kept her going, excited her and intrigued her with the various possibilities it offered. For she would not die here like an animal breathing its last in a corner; she wanted an aura of the mysterious and mystical to hover around her death. She would come to a heroic, legendary end like the queens of antiquity. Her life had burned bright, and so must her death; it must arouse the somnolent admiration of the multitude once again. No one in Paris was to guess that she died here in torment, choked by loneliness and disfavour, burnt up by her unsatisfied greed for power; she would deceive them all by staging her death as a drama. Deception, the delight of her life, opened up her heart again. She would end it all in a blazing fire of merriment, as if at random, she wouldn't die squirming like a discarded wax taper coiling on the ground, trodden out in pity. She would go down into the abyss dancing.

Next day a number of notes flew away from her desk:

affectionate, appealing, seductive, imperious, promising and softly perfumed lines. She scattered her invitations around Paris and the provinces, she held out the prospect of their favourite occupations to everyone, offered some hunting, others gaming, others again masked balls. She had actors, singers and dancers hired by her agents in Paris, she ordered expensive costumes, announced the founding of a second court in France, with all the refinements and pleasures of Versailles. She enticed and invited strangers and acquaintances, the distinguished and the less distinguished, but she must have people here, a great many people, an audience for the comedy of happiness and satisfaction that she was going to stage before the end came.

And soon a new life began in Courbépine. Parisian society, always craving pleasure, sought out this novelty. In addition, its members all felt a secret, slightly contemptuous curiosity to see how the former mistress of France, now toppled, took her exile. One festivity followed another. Carriages came emblazoned with noble coats of arms, large country coaches arrived crammed with high-spirited passengers, army officers came on horseback—more visitors flooded in every day, and with them an army of hangers-on and servants. Many had brought pastoral costumes with them, as if for a rustic game, others came in great pomp and ceremony. The little village was like a military camp.

And the château awoke, its once unlighted windows shining proudly, for it was enlivened by talking and laughter, games and music. People walked up and down, couples whispered in corners where only grey silence had lurked. Women's dresses glowed in bright hues in the shade of the shrubberies, the cheerfully plangent tunes of risqué songs were plucked on mandolins far into the night. Servants hurried along the corridors, the windows were framed by flowers, coloured lights sparkled among the bushes. They lived out the carefree life of Versailles, the light charm of heedlessness. The absence of the real court did take a little of the bloom off it all, but increased the exuberance that encouraged the guests to dance, free from all constraints of etiquette.

At the centre of this whirlwind of activity, madame de Prie felt her sluggish blood begin to circulate feverishly again. She was one of those women, and they are not rare, who are shaped entirely by other people's attitudes. She was beautiful when she was desired, witty in clever company, proud when she was flattered, in love when she was loved. The more that was expected of her, the more she gave. But in solitude, where no one saw her, spoke to her, heard her or wanted anything of her, she had become ugly, dull-witted, helpless, unhappy. She could be lively only in the midst of life; in isolation she dwindled to a shadow. And now that the reflected light of her earlier life shone around her, all her merriment and her carefree charm sparkled in the air again, she was witty once more, agreeable, she wove her enchantments, made conversation, caught fire from the glances that lingered on her. She forgot that she meant to deceive these people with her cheerfulness, and was in genuine high spirits, she took every smile as a piece of good fortune, every word as true, plunged feverishly into enjoying the company she had been deprived of so long, as if falling into the arms of a lover.

She made the festivities wilder and wilder, she summoned more and more guests, enticing them to Courbépine. And more and more came. For at the time, after the failure of John Law's financial system, the land was impoverished, but she herself was rich, and she was casting the millions she had extorted during her time of power to the wind. Money was thrown down on the gaming tables, went up in smoke in expensive firework displays, was squandered on exotic fancies, but she threw it away more and more wildly, like a woman desperate. The guests were amazed, surprised by her lavish expenditure and the magnificence of the festivities; no one knew in whose honour they were really given. And in all the wild merriment, she herself almost forgot.

The festivities continued unabated for the whole month of August. September came, the trees wore colourful fruits in their hair, and the evening clouds were shot with gold. The guests were fewer now; time was pressing.

But amidst the pleasures, madame de Prie had almost forgotten her purpose. Wishing to deceive others with such magnificent frenzies, she deceived herself; her carefree mood matched this imitation of her former life so well that she took it for real, and even believed in her power, her beauty, her *joie de vivre*.

To be sure, one thing was different, and that hurt. People were all kinder to her now that she was of no importance, they were warmer and yet cooler. The women no longer envied her, did not inflict malicious little pinpricks, the men did not flock around her. They all laughed with her, treated her as a good friend, but they told no more lies about love, they did not beg, they did not flatter, they did not make an enemy of her, and that was what made her feel that she was quite powerless. A life without envy, hatred and lies was not a life worth living. She realised, with horror, that in fact she had already been forgotten; the social whirl was as wild as ever, but she was not at its centre now. The men laughed with other women, whose freshness and youth they saw for the first time; the moment had come to remind the world of herself again before she grew old and a stranger to them all.

She put off her decision from day to day. A sensation quivered within her, half fear, half hope that something might yet hold her back, might keep her from that despairing leap into the irrevocable. Among all those pairs of hands reaching for the food on her tables, holding women close in the dance, rolling gold coins over the gaming tables, might there not be one who could hold her back, would want to hold her back, one who loved her so much that she could happily dispense with the bright show of a large company, and exchange the unstable possession of royal power for him? Without knowing it, she was looking for such a thing; she courted the passion of all the men, for she was courting her own life. But they all passed her by.

Then, one day, she met a young captain in the royal guard, a handsome, amusing fellow whom she had noticed before. They met as twilight fell over the park, and she saw him walking up and down among the trees, his eyes wild, his teeth clenched, and sometimes he struck the tree trunks with his fist. She spoke to him. He gave her a distracted answer; she saw that some secret was troubling him, and asked the reason for his desperation. At last he confessed that he had lost a hundred *louis d'or* at the gaming table, money entrusted to him by his regiment. That made him a thief, and now he must carry out sentence on himself. She felt it strangely ominous that here, amidst this happy tumult, someone else had come to the same dark conclusion too. But this man was young, had rosy cheeks, could laugh again; there was still help for him. She summoned him to her room and gave him five hundred *louis d'or*. Trembling with joy, he kissed her hands. She kept him there a long time, but that was all he wanted from her, he asked no more with any glance or gesture. She was shaken; she couldn't even buy love now. That fortified her in her decision.

She sent him away, and stepped quickly out into the hall. Laughter met her as she opened the door, happy voices and lively people filled the room like a cloud. Suddenly she felt that she hated them all, cheerful as they were, dancing and laughing on her grave. Envy took hold of her when she thought that they would all live on, and be happy.

She was burning with a malicious desire to disturb her guests, alarm and confuse them, stop their laughter. And suddenly, when their exuberance died down for a second and silence fell, she said directly, "Don't you notice that there's a death in the house?"

For a moment confusion reigned. Even to a drunk, the word 'death' is like a hammer falling on his heart. Baffled, they asked each other who was dead. "I am," madame de Prie said coldly, without any change of expression, "I shall not see this winter come."

She spoke so gravely, in so sombre a tone, that they all looked at one another in silence. But only for a second. Then a jest flew from somewhere in the room like a coloured ball, someone else threw it back, and as if enlivened by the curious notion of death the wave of exuberance surged foaming and high again, and buried the discomfort of that initial surprise.

Madame de Prie remained very calm. She felt that there was no going back now. But it amused her to stage her prophecy even more dramatically. She went up to one of the round tables where her guests were playing faro, and waited for the next card to be turned over. It was a seven of one of the black suits, clubs or spades. "The seventh of October, then." Without meaning to, she had said it out loud under her breath.

"What's the seventh of October?" one of the onlookers asked casually.

She looked at him calmly. "The day of my death."

They all laughed. The joke was passed on. Madame de Prie was delighted to find that no one believed her. If they didn't trust her in life any more, then at least they should see how she and her comedy had fooled them in death. A wonderful sense of superiority, pleasure and ease ran through her limbs. She felt as if she must re-joice aloud in high spirits and derision.

In the next room music was playing. A dance had just begun. She joined the dancers, and had never danced better.

From that moment on, her life had meaning again. She knew she was preparing to do something that would certainly make her immortal. She imagined the King's amazement, the horror of her guests when her prophecy of her death came true to the very day. And she was staging the comedy most carefully; she invited more and more guests, doubled her expenditure, worked on the multifarious magnificence of these last days as if it were a work of art, something that would make her sudden fall even more keenly felt. She aired the prediction of her death again at every opportunity, but always drew a glittering curtain of merriment over it; she wanted everyone to know that it had been announced, and no one to believe it. Only death would raise her name once again to the ranks of those who could never be forgotten, from which the King had cast her down.

Two days before she was to carry out her irrevocable purpose, she gave the last and most magnificent festivities of all. Since the Persian and other Islamic embassies had set up for the first time in Paris, all things Oriental had been the fashion in France: books were written in Eastern guise, the fairy tales and legends of the Orient were translated, Arab costume was popular, and people imitated the flowery style of Eastern language. At enormous expense, madame de Prie had turned the whole château into an Oriental palace. Costly rugs lay on the floor, squawking parrots and white-feathered cockatoos rocked on their perches on the window bars, held there by silver chains; servants hurried soundlessly down the corridors in turbans and baggy silk trousers, taking Turkish sweetmeats and other refreshments entirely unknown at the time to the guests, who were dazzled by such daring splendour. Coloured tents were erected in the garden, boys cooled them by waving broad fans, music rang out from the dark shadows of the shrubberies, everything possible was done to make the evening an unforgettable fairy-tale experience, and the silvery half-moon hanging in the starry sky that night encouraged the imagination to conjure up the mysteriously sultry atmosphere of a night by the Bosphorus.

But the real surprise was a particularly spacious tent, containing a stage hung with red velvet curtains. Wishing to appear to her guests in the full radiance of her fame and beauty, madame de Prie had decided to act a play herself; a final display of all the merriment and levity of her life to an audience was to be her last and finest deception. In the few days she still had left, she had commissioned a young author to write a play to her exact requirements. Time was short and his alexandrines bad, but that was not what mattered to her. The tragedy was set in the Orient, and she herself was to play the part of Zengane, a young queen whose realm is captured by enemies and who goes proudly to her death, although the magnanimous victor offers to share all his royal power with her if she will be his wife. She had insisted on these details: she wanted to give a dress rehearsal of her voluntary death in front of the unsuspecting audience before she put the plan into practice.

And in addition she wanted to experience the past once more, if only in game, she wanted to be queen again, and show that she was born to it and must die once she was deprived of power.

Her aim was to be beautiful and royal in the eyes of others on that last evening; she would adorn her past image with an invisible crown, ensuring that her name aroused that pure shiver of veneration which attends all that is sublime. Cosmetics veiled the pallor of her sunken cheeks, her thin figure was concealed by the flowing Oriental robes she wore, the confusing brightness of the jewels gleaming on her hair, like dew on a dark flower in the morning moisture, outshone her tired eyes. And when she appeared like this in the brightness behind the curtain as it swept back, a brightness further intensified by her passion, when she appeared on stage surrounded by kneeling servants and the awe-stricken populace, a rustle passed through the ranks of her guests. Her heart was thudding: for the first time in these bitter weeks she felt the delightful wave of admiration that had borne her life up for so long surging towards her, and a wonderful feeling arose in her, a sweet sadness mingled with melancholy pleasure, a regret that kept receding, flowing back into a great sense of happiness. Before her, the surf of the wave flickered, she did not see individuals any more, only a great crowd, perhaps her guests, perhaps all France, perhaps generations yet to come, perhaps eternity. And she felt only, and blissfully, one thing: she was standing on a great height again, envied, admired, the cynosure of all those curious and nameless eyes, and at last, after such a long time, she felt aware of living again, of being really alive. Death was not too high a price to pay for this second of life.

She played her part magnificently, although she had never tried acting before. She had shed everything that prevents most people from making a show of emotion to others—fear, timidity, shame, awkwardness—she had shed all that, and was now playing only with objects. She wanted to be queen, and she was queen again for the length of an hour. Only once did her breath fail her, when she spoke the line, *"Je vais mourir, oh ne me plaignez pas!"** , for she felt that she was expressing her deep wish for life, and was afraid they might not be deceived, might understand her, warn her, hold her back. But in fact the pause after that cry seemed in itself to be acted with such irresistible credibility that a shudder ran through the audience. And when, with a wild gesture, she turned the dagger against her heart, fell, and seemed to die smiling, when the play was over—although only now did it really begin—they stormed to applaud her, paying her tribute with an enthusiasm that she had not known even in the days of her greatest power.

---

* Now I shall die, oh do not mourn for me

However, she had only a smile for all the uproar, and when she was complimented on her magnificent performance of the death of Zengane, she said calmly, "I suppose that, today, I should know how to die. Death dwells in me already. It will all be over the day after tomorrow."

They laughed again, but it no longer hurt her. There was blessed, painless merriment inside her, and such a childishly exuberant joy at having deceived all these enthusiastic people that she instinctively joined in the peals of laughter. Once she had played only with men and power; now she saw that there was no better toy than death.

Next day, the last full day of her life, the guests went away; she meant to receive death alone. The coaches churned up white dust like clouds in the distance, the horsemen trotted away, the halls were emptied of light and laughter, a restless wind howled down the chimney. She felt as if the blood were slowly flowing out of her veins with the departing guests, she felt herself becoming colder and colder, weaker, more defenceless, more fearful. Death had seemed to her so easy yesterday, just a game; now that she was alone again, it suddenly showed her its horror and its power once more.

And everything that she thought she had tamed and trodden underfoot awoke again. The last evening came, and once more the snake-like shadows that, alarmed by the light, had hidden behind objects came crawling out of hiding with flickering tongues. Dread, stifled by laughter and veiled by the bright images of human company, gradually returned all-powerful to the deserted rooms. The silence had only been cowering under the surging sound of voices; now it spread abroad again like mist, filled the rooms, the halls, the stairways, the corridors, and her shuddering heart as well.

She would have liked to make an end of it at once. But she had chosen the seventh of October, and must not destroy the deception, that artificial, glimmering, lying construct of her triumph, just for the sake of a whim. She must wait. It was worse than being dead, though, to wait for the hour of death while the wind outside mocked her, and dark shadows in here reached for her heart. How could she bear this long last night before death, this endless time until dawn? Dark objects, spectre-like, pressed closer and closer, all the shades of her past life rose from their burial vaults—she fled before them from room to room, but they stared at her from the pictures, grinned behind the windows, crouched down behind cupboards. The dead reached out to her, though she was still alive and wanted human company, company just for one night. She longed for a human being as if for a coat in which to wrap her shivering form until day dawned.

Suddenly she rang the bell, which screeched shrilly like a wounded animal. A servant, drowsy with sleep, came upstairs to her. She told him to go at once to the priest's nephew, wake him and bring him here. She had important news for him.

The servant stared as if she were mad. But she did not feel it, she felt nothing at all, every emotion had died in her. She was not ashamed to summon the man who had beaten her, she did not hesitate to summon a man to her bedroom at night in front of the servant. There was only a cold void in her, she felt that her poor shivering body needed warmth if it were not to freeze. Her soul was dead already; she had only to kill her body now.

After a while the door opened. Her former lover came in. His face was chilly and contemptuous, he seemed unspeakably strange to her. And yet the horror shrank back slightly under the objects in the room, just because he opened the door and she was no longer entirely alone with them.

He took pains to seem very decided and not betray his inner astonishment, since this summons was entirely unexpected. For days, while the festivities were in full swing in the château, he had slunk around the barred gateways of the park, his eyes narrowed with rage; he had eaten his heart out with self-reproaches, for he, as her lover, should have been able to stride through the midst of this brilliance. He was consumed with anger for having so humiliated her; those extravagant festivities had suddenly made the power of the wealth that he had failed to exploit very clear to him again. And moreover, his hours with madame de Prie had made him desire these fine, fragrant, spoilt ladies with their delicate, fragile limbs, their strangely provocative lusts, their rustling silken dresses. He had taken himself back to the priest's poverty-stricken house, where everything suddenly seemed to him crude, dirty and worn. His greed, once roused, made him look avidly at all the ladies who came from Paris, but none of them looked back at him, their coaches scornfully splashed him with the mud their wheels threw up, and the great lords didn't even see him when he humbly raised his hat to them. A hundred times he had felt impelled to go into the château and fling himself at madame de Prie's feet, and every time fear had held him back.

But now she had summoned him, and that made him arrogant. Inwardly, he straightened his back: it was the proudest moment of his life to think that she needed him again after all.

For a moment they looked at one another, barely able to hide the hatred in their eyes. At that moment, each despised the other because each intended to misuse the other. Madame de Prie controlled herself. Her voice was very cool.

"The Duke of Berlington asked me yesterday if I could recommend him a secretary. If you would like the post, I'll send you to Paris tomorrow with a letter for him.'

The young man trembled. He had already assumed a haughty bearing, intending to be condescending and gracious if she was seeking his favours. But all that was gone now. Greed overcame him. Paris gleamed before his eyes.

"If madame were to be so kind—I—I can't think of anything that would make me happier," he stammered. His eyes had the pleading expression of a beaten dog in them.

She nodded. Then she looked at him, commandingly yet milder again. He understood. Everything would be the way it had once been ...

And not for a second of that passionate night did she forget that she hated him, despised him, and was deceiving him—for there was no Duke of Berlington —she knew how contemptible she herself was, driven to buy a man's caresses with a lie, yet it was life, real life that she felt in his limbs, drank from his lips, not the darkness and silence already coming to hold her fast. She felt the warmth of his youth driving death away, and knew at every moment that she was trying to deceive death itself, the death that was coming closer and closer, and of whose power she now, for the first time, had some inkling.

The morning of the seventh of October was clear. Sunlight shimmered above the fields, even the shadows were translucent and pure. Madame de Prie dressed carefully, as if for a great feast, put her affairs in order, burned letters. She locked her jewellery, which was very valuable, in an ebony casket, tore up all her promissory notes and contracts. Now that it was day again, everything in her was clear and determined once more, and she wanted clarity above all else.

Her lover came in. She spoke to him kindly and without resentment; it pained her to think that she was so pitilessly deceiving the last man who had meant anything to her, even if he had not meant much. She did not want anyone to speak of her with resentment, only with admiration and gratitude. And she felt an urge to lavish the jewellery from the casket on him, in return for that one last night. It was a fortune.

But he was half-asleep and inattentive. In his boorish greed for gain, he thought of nothing but his position, his future. The memory of their passionate caresses made him yet bolder. Abruptly, he said he must set off for Paris at once, or he might arrive too late, and he demanded rather than requested the letter of recommendation. Something froze inside her. She had hired him, and now he was asking for payment.

She wrote the letter, a letter to a man who did not exist and whom he could never find. But she still hesitated to give it to him. Once more she put off her decision. She asked if he couldn't stay one day longer; she would like that very much, she said. And as she spoke she balanced the casket in her hand. She felt that if he said yes it might yet save her. But all their decisions led the same way. He was in a hurry. He didn't want to stay. If he had not said it in such a surly manner, making her feel so clearly that he had let himself be bought only for one night, she would have given him the jewellery, which was worth hundreds of thousands of livres. But he was brusque, his glance impudent and with no love in it. So she took a single, very small jewel with only a dull glow to it—dull as his eyes—and gave it to him in return for taking the casket, of whose contents he had no idea, to the Ursuline convent in Paris. She added a letter asking the nuns to say Masses for her soul. Then she sent the impatient young man off to find the Duke of Berlington.

He thanked her, not effusively, and left, unaware of the value of the casket that he himself was carrying. And so, after acting out a comedy of her feelings in front of them all, she deceived even the last man to cross her path.

Then she closed the door and quickly took a small flask from a drawer. It was made of fine Chinese porcelain, with strange, monstrous dragons coiling and curling in blue on it. She looked at it with curiosity, toyed with it as carelessly as she had toyed with her fellow men and women, with princes, with France, with love and death. She unscrewed the stopper and poured the clear liquid into a small dish. For a moment she hesitated, really just from a childish fear that it might have a bitter flavour.

Cautiously, like a kitten sniffing warm milk, she touched it with her tongue; no, it didn't taste bad. And so she drank the contents of the dish down in a single draught.

The whole thing, at that moment, seemed to her somehow amusing and extremely ludicrous: to think that you had only to take that one tiny sip, and tomorrow you wouldn't see the clouds, the fields, the woods any more, messengers would go riding, the King would be horrified and all of France amazed. So this was the great step that she had feared taking so much. She thought of the astonishment of her guests, of the legends that would be told of the way she had foretold the day of her death, and failed to understand only one thing: that she had given herself to death because she missed the company of humans, those same gullible humans who could be deceived with such a little comedy. Dying seemed to her altogether easy, you could even smile as you died—yes, you could indeed, she tried it—you could perfectly well smile, and it wasn't difficult to preserve a beautiful and tranquil face in death, a face radiant with unearthly bliss. It was true, even after death you could act happiness. She hadn't known that. She found everything, human beings, the world, death and life suddenly so very amusing that the smile she had prepared sprang involuntarily to her carefree lips. She straightened up, as if there were a mirror opposite her somewhere, waited for death, and smiled and smiled and smiled.

But death was not to be deceived, and broke her laughter. When madame de Prie was found her face was distorted into a terrible grimace. Those dreadful features showed everything that she had really suffered in the last few weeks: her rage, her torment, her aimless fear, her wild and desperate pain. The deceptive smile for which she had struggled so avidly had been helpless, had drained away. Her feet were twisted together in torment, her hands had clutched a curtain so convulsively that scraps of it were left between her fingers, her mouth was open as if in a shrill scream.

And all that show of apparent merriment, the mystic prophecy of the day of her death had been for nothing too. The news of her suicide arrived in Paris on the evening when an Italian conjuror was displaying his arts at court. He made rabbits disappear into a hat, he brought grown geese out of eggshells. When the message arrived people were slightly interested, were surprised, whispered, the name of madame de Prie went around for a few minutes, but then the conjuror performed another amazing trick and she was forgotten, just as she herself would have forgotten someone else's fate at such a moment. Interest in her strange end did not last long in France, and her desperate efforts to stage a drama that would never be forgotten were in vain. The fame she longed for, the immortality she thought to seize by force with her death, passed her name by: her story was buried under the dust and ashes of trivial events. For the history of the world will not tolerate intruders; it chooses its own heroes and implacably dismisses those not summoned to that rank, however hard they may try; someone who has fallen off the carriage of fate as it goes along will never catch up with it again. And nothing was left of the strange end of madame de Prie, her real life and the ingeniously devised deception of her death but a few dry lines in some book of memoirs or other, conveying to their reader as little of the passionate emotions of her life as a pressed flower allows one to guess at the fragrant marvel of its long-forgotten spring.

MOONBEAM ALLEY

THE SHIP, delayed by a storm, could not land at the small French seaport until late in the evening, and I missed the night train to Germany. So I had an unexpected day to spend in this foreign town, and an evening which offered nothing more alluring than the melancholy music of a ladies' ensemble in a suburban nightclub, or a tedious conversation with my chance-met travelling companions. The air in the small hotel dining-room seemed to me intolerable, greasy with oil, stifling with smoke, and I suffered doubly from its murky impurity because I still tasted the pure breath of the sea on my lips, cool and salty. So I went out and walked down the broad, brightly lit street, going nowhere in particular, until I reached a square where an outdoor band was playing. I went on amidst the casually flowing tide of people who were out for a stroll. At first it did me good to be carried passively away by this current of provincially dressed persons who meant nothing to me, but soon I could no longer tolerate the company of strangers surging up close to me with their disconnected laughter, their eyes resting on me in surprise, with odd looks or a grin, the touches that imperceptibly urged me on, the light coming from a thousand small sources, the constant sound of footsteps. The sea voyage had been turbulent, and I still felt a reeling, slightly intoxicated sensation in my blood, a rocking and gliding beneath my feet, the earth seemed to move as if it were breathing and the street to rise to the sky. All this loud confusion suddenly made me dizzy, and to save myself I turned into a side street without looking at its name, and then into a yet smaller street, where the senseless noise gradually ebbed away. I walked aimlessly on through the tangle of alleys branching off each other like veins, and becoming darker and darker the further I went from the main square. The large electrical arc lamps that lit the broad avenues like moons did not shine here, and the stars at last began coming into view again above the few street lamps, in a black and partly overcast sky.

I must have reached the sailors' quarter near the harbour. I could tell from the smell of rotting fish, from the sweetish aroma of seaweed and decay that bladder-wrack gives off when the breakers wash it ashore, from the typical fumes of pollution and unaired rooms that linger dankly in these nooks and crannies until a great storm rises, bringing in fresh air. The nebulous darkness and unexpected solitude did me good. I slowed my pace, glancing down alley after alley now, each different from its neighbour, here a quiet alley, there an inviting one, but all dark, with the muted sound of music and voices rising so mysteriously from invisible vaults that one could scarcely guess at its underground sources. For the doors to all the cellars were closed, with only the light of a red or yellow lamp showing.

I liked such alleyways in foreign towns, places that are a disreputable market-place for all the passions, a secret accumulation of temptations for the sailors who, after many lonely days on strange and dangerous seas, come here for just one night to fulfil all their many sensuous dreams within an hour. These little side-streets have to lurk somewhere in the poorer part of any big city, lying low, because they say so boldly and importunately things that are hidden beneath a hundred disguises in the brightly lit buildings with their shining window panes and distinguished denizens. Enticing music wafts from small rooms here, garish cinematograph posters promise unimaginable splendours, small square lanterns hang under gateways, winking in very clear invitation, issuing an intimate greeting, and naked flesh glimpsed through a door left ajar shimmers under gilded fripperies. Drunks shout in the bars, gamblers argue in loud voices. The sailors grin when they meet each other here, their dull eyes glinting in anticipation, for they can find everything in such places, women and gaming, drink and a show to watch, adventures both grubby and great. But all this is hidden in modestly muted yet tell-tale fashion behind shutters lowered for the look of the thing, it all goes on behind closed doors, and that apparent seclusion is intriguing, is twice as seductive because it is both hidden and accessible. Such streets are the same in Hamburg and Colombo and Havana, similar in all seaports, just as the wide and luxurious avenues resemble each other, for the upper side and underside of life share the same form. These shady streets are the last fantastic remnants of a sensually unregulated world where instinct still has free rein, brutal and unbridled; they are a dark wood of passions, a thicket full of the animal kingdom, exciting visitors with what they reveal and enticing them with what they hide. One can weave them into dreams.

And the alley where I suddenly felt myself a captive was such a street. I had been idly following a couple of cuirassiers whose swords, dragging along after them, clinked on the uneven road surface. Women called to them from a bar, they laughed and shouted coarse jests back at the girls, one of the soldiers knocked at the window, then a voice somewhere swore at them and they went on. Their laughter faded in the distance, and soon they were out of my hearing. The alley was silent again; a couple of windows shone faintly, mistily reflecting the pale moon. I stood drinking in that silence, which struck me as a strange one because something behind it seemed to be murmuring words of mystery, lust and danger. I clearly felt that the silence was deceptive, and something of the world's decay shimmered in the murky haze. But I went on standing there, listening to the empty air. I was no longer aware of the town and the alley, of their

74

names or my own, I just sensed that I was a stranger here, miraculously detached in the unknown, with no purpose in mind, no message to deliver, no links with anything, and yet I sensed all the dark life around me as fully as I felt the blood flowing beneath my own skin. I had only the impression that nothing here was for me and yet it all was all mine: it was the delightful sensation of an experience made deepest and most genuine because one is not personally involved. That sensation is one of the well-springs of my inmost being, and in an unknown situation it always comes over me like desire. Then suddenly, as I stood listening in the lonely alley as if waiting for something that was bound to happen, something to urge me on, out of this somnambulistic sensation of listening to the void, I heard, muted by either distance or a wall between us, the very faint sound of a song in German coming from somewhere. It was that simple air from *Der Freischütz*, "Fairest, greenest bridal wreath." A woman's voice was singing it, very badly, but it was still a German tune, something German here in a foreign part of the world, and so it affected me in a way all its own. It was being sung some way off, but I felt it like a greeting, the first word I had heard in my native tongue for weeks. Who, I asked myself, speaks my language here, whose memory impels her to lift her voice from the heart in singing this poor little song here in this remote, disreputable alley? I followed the voice, going from house to house. They all stood half asleep, their shutters closed, but light shining behind the shutters gave their nature away, and sometimes a hand waved. Outside there were garish signs, screaming posters, and the words "Ale, Whisky, Beer" promised a hidden bar, but it all appeared sealed and uninviting, yet enticing at the same time. Now and then—and I heard a few footsteps in the distance—now and then the voice came again, singing the refrain more clearly this time, sounding closer and closer. I identified the house. For a moment I hesitated, and then pushed my foot against the inner door, which was heavily draped with white net curtains. However, as I stooped to go in, having made up my mind, something came to life in the shadow of the entrance and gave a start of alarm, a figure that had obviously been waiting there, its face pressed close to the pane. The lantern over the door cast red light on that face, yet it was pale with fright—a man was staring at me, wide-eyed. He muttered something like an apology and disappeared down the dimly lit alley. It was a strange greeting. I looked the way he had gone. Something still seemed to be moving in the vanishing shadows of the alley, but indistinctly. Inside the building the voice was still singing, and seemed to me even clearer now. That lured me on. I turned the door-handle and quickly stepped inside.

The last word of the song stopped short, as if cut off

by a knife. And in some alarm I felt a void before me, a sense of silent hostility as if I had broken something. Only slowly did my eyes adjust to the room, which was almost empty: it contained a bar counter and a table, and the whole place was obviously just a means of access to other rooms behind it, whose real purpose was immediately made obvious by their opened doors, muted lamplight, and beds made up and ready. A girl sat at the table, leaning her elbows on it, her tired face made up, and behind her at the bar was the landlady, stout and dingy grey, with another girl who was not bad-looking. My greeting sounded harsh in the space, and a bored response came back with some delay. Finding that I had stepped into such a void, so tense and bleak a silence, I was ill at ease and would rather have left at once, but in my embarrassment I could think of no excuse, so I resigned myself to sitting down at the table in front of the bar. The girl, remembering her duties, asked what I would like to drink, and I recognised her as German at once from the harsh accent of her French. I ordered beer, she went out and came back again with the lethargic bearing that betrayed even more indifference than the empty look in her eyes, which glowed faintly under their lids like lights going out. Automatically, and in accordance with the custom of such places, she put a second glass down next to mine for herself. As she raised her glass she did not turn her blank gaze on me, so I was able to observe her. Her face was in fact still beautiful, with regular features, but inner weariness seemed to make it coarse, like a mask; everything about her drooped, her eyelids were heavy, her hair hung loose, her cheeks, badly made up and smudged, were already beginning to fall in, and broad lines ran down to her mouth. Her dress too was carelessly draped, her voice hoarse, roughened by smoke and beer. All things considered, I felt that this was an exhausted woman who went on living only out of habit and without feelings, so to speak. Self-consciously and with a sense of dread I asked a question. She replied with dull indifference, scarcely moving her lips, and without looking at me. I felt I was unwelcome. At the back of the room the landlady was yawning, and the other girl was sitting in a corner glancing in my direction, as if waiting for me to summon her. I would have liked to leave, but everything about me felt heavy, and I sat in that sated, smouldering air swaying slightly as the sailors do, kept there by both distaste and curiosity, for this indifference was, in a way, intriguing.

Then I suddenly gave a start, alarmed by raucous laughter near me. At the same time the flame of the light wavered, and the draught told me that someone must have opened the door behind my back. "Oh, so here you are again, are you?" said the voice beside me shrilly, in German. "Slinking round the house again, you skinflint? Well, come along in, I won't hurt you."

I spun round, to look first at her as she uttered this greeting, in tones as piercing as if her body had suddenly caught fire, then at the door. Even before it was fully open I recognised the trembling figure and humble glance of the man who had been almost glued to the outside of the pane just now. Intimidated, he held his hat in his hand like a beggar, trembling at the sound of the raucous greeting and the laughter which suddenly seemed to shake her apathetic figure convulsively, and which was accompanied by the landlady's rapid whispering from the bar counter at the back of the room.

"Sit down there with Françoise, then," the woman beside me ordered the poor man as he came closer with a craven, shuffling step. "You can see I have a gentleman here."

She said this to him in German. The landlady and the other girl laughed out loud, although they couldn't understand her, but they seemed to know the new guest.

"Give him champagne, Françoise, the expensive brand, give him a bottle of it!" she called out, laughing, and turning to him again added with derision, "And if it's too expensive for you then you can stay outside, you miserable miser. I suppose you'd like to stare at me for free—you want everything for free, don't you?"

The tall figure seemed almost to collapse at the sound

of this vicious laughter; he hunched his back as if his face were trying to creep away and hide like a dog, and his hand shook as he reached for the bottle and spilled some of the wine in pouring it. He was still trying to look up at her face, but he could not lift his gaze from the floor, where it wandered over the tiles. And only now, in the lamplight, did I clearly see that emaciated face, worn and pale, his hair damp and thin on his bony skull, his joints loose and looking as if they were broken, a pitiful creature without any strength, yet not devoid of malice. Everything about him was crooked, awry, cringing, and now, when he raised his eyes, though he immediately lowered them again in alarm, they had a gleam of ill-will in them.

"Don't trouble yourself about him!" the girl told me in French, roughly taking my arm as if to turn me round. "This is old business between the two of us, it's nothing new." And again, baring her teeth as if ready to bite, she called out to him, "Listen to me, you old lynx! You just hear what I say. I said I'd rather jump into the sea than go with you, didn't I?"

Once again the landlady and the other girl laughed, loud and foolish laughter. It seemed to be a familiar joke to them, a daily jest. But I found it unpleasant to see that other girl, Françoise, suddenly press close to him with pretended affection, wheedling him with flattery from which he shrank, though he didn't have the courage to shake her off, and I was alarmed when his wandering gaze, awkward, anxious, abject, rested on me. And I felt dread of the woman beside me, who had suddenly been roused from her apathy and was full of such burning malice that her hands trembled. I threw some money on the table and was going to leave, but she wouldn't take it.

"If he annoys you I'll throw him out, the bastard. He must do as he's told. Come along, drink another glass with me!"

She pressed close to me with a wild, abrupt kind of tenderness which I knew at once was only pretended, to torment the other man. At every movement she quickly looked askance across the table, and it was dreadful to me to see how he began to wince whenever she paid me some little attention, as if he felt hot steel branding his flesh. Without paying any attention to her, I stared only at him, and shuddered to see something in the nature of anger, rage, envy and greed arising in him, yet he cringed again if she so much as turned her head. She now pressed very close to me, her body trembling with her vicious pleasure in this game, and I felt horror at her garishly painted face with its smell of cheap powder, at the fumes emanating from her slack flesh. I reached for a cigar to keep her away from my face, and while my eyes were searching the table for a match she ordered him, "Bring us a light!"

I was more horrified than he was at such an imposition, making him serve me, and quickly set about looking for a light myself. But he snapped to attention at her words as if at the crack of a whip, came over to us, reeling, with unsteady footsteps, and put his own lighter on the table quickly, as if he might burn up if he touched the table-top. For a second I met his eyes: there was boundless shame in them, and crushing embitterment. That servile glance of his struck a chord in me as another man, a brother. I felt the force of his humiliation at the woman's hands and was ashamed for him.

"Thank you very much," I said in German—she start-ed at that—"but you shouldn't have troubled." Then I offered him my hand. A hesitation, a long one, then I felt damp, bony fingers, and suddenly, convulsively, an abrupt pressure in thanks. For a second his eyes shone as they looked at mine, and then they were hidden again by those slack eyelids. In defiance of the woman, I was going to ask him to sit down with us, and I must already have begun to trace the gesture of invitation, for she quickly ordered him, "You sit down again and don't dis-turb us here."

All at once I was overcome by disgust at the sound of her caustic voice and this scene of torture. What did I care for this smoky bar, this unpleasant whore and the feeble man, these fumes of beer, smoke and cheap perfume? I craved fresh air. I pushed the money over to her, stood up and moved away with decision as she came flatteringly closer to me. It revolted me to help her humiliate another human being, and the determined manner of my withdrawal clearly showed how little she attracted me sensually. Her blood was up now, a line appeared around her mouth, but whatever word sprang to her lips she took care not to utter it, just turning on him and flouncing with undisguised hatred. But he was expecting the worst, and at this threatening move-ment he rapidly, with a hunted look, put his hand in his pocket and brought out a purse. It was obvious that he was afraid of being left alone with her now, and in his haste he had trouble untying the purse-strings—it was the kind of knitted purse adorned with glass beads that peasants and the lower classes carry. Anyone could see that he wasn't used to throwing his money about, un-like the sailors who produce the coins clinking in their pockets with a sweeping gesture and fling them down on the table; he was clearly in the habit of counting money carefully and weighing the coins up in his fingers. "How he trembles for his dear, sweet *pfennigs!* Are we going too slowly for you? Wait!" she mocked, and came a step closer. He shrank back, and seeing his alarm she said, shrugging her shoulders and with unspeakable revulsion in her eyes, "Oh, I won't take anything from you, I spit on your money. I know you've counted all your dear, nice little *pfennigs.* No one in the world must have too much money. And then of course," she added, suddenly tapping his chest, "there's the banknotes you've sewn in there so that no one will steal them!"

Sure enough, like a man with a weak heart suddenly clutching at his breast, he reached with a pale and trembling hand for a certain place on his coat, his fingers instinctively felt for the secret hiding-place and came away again, reassured. "Miser!" she spat. But then, suddenly, a flush rose to her victim's face; he threw the purse abruptly at the other girl, who first cried out in alarm, then laughed aloud, and he stormed past her and out of the door as if escaping from a fire.

For a moment she still stood there, eyes flashing with fury. Then her eyelids fell apathetically again, weariness relaxed her body from its tension. She seemed to grow old and tired within a moment. Something uncertain and lost blurred the gaze now resting on me. She stood there like a drunk waking up, feeling numb and empty with shame. "He'll be weeping and wailing for his money outside. Maybe he'll go to the police and say we stole it. And he'll be back tomorrow, but he won't have me all the same. Anyone else can, but not him!"

She went to the bar, threw coins down on it and swallowed a glass of brandy in a single draught. The vicious light was back in her eyes, but blurred as if by tears of rage and shame. I felt nauseated by her, and that destroyed pity. "Good evening," I said, and left. *"Bonsoir,"* replied the landlady. She did not look round but just laughed, shrill and scornful laughter.

When I stepped outside there was nothing in the alley but night and the sky, a sultry darkness with the moonlight veiled and endlessly far away. I greedily took great breaths of the warm yet reviving air, my sense of dread turned to amazement at the diversity of human fate, and I felt again—it is a feeling that can make me happy to the point of tears—how fate is always waiting behind every window, every door opens on new experience, the wide variety of this world is omnipresent, and even its dirtiest corners swarm with predestined events as if with the iridescent gleam of beetles decomposing. Gone was the distasteful part of the encounter, and my tension was pleasantly resolved, turning to a sweet weariness that longed to turn all I had just seen and heard into a more attractive dream. Instinctively I looked around me, trying to work out my way back through this tangle of winding alleys. Then a shadow—he must have come close without making any noise—approached me.

"Forgive me,"—and I immediately recognised that humble tone of voice—"but I don't think you know your way around here. May I—may I show you which way to go? You are staying, sir, at … ?"

I told him the name of my hotel.

"I'll go with you … if you'll permit me," he immediately added humbly.

Dread came over me again. This stealthy, spectral step, almost soundless yet close beside me, the darkness of the sailors' alley and the memory of what I had just witnessed all gradually turned to a dreamlike confusion of the emotions, leaving me devoid of judgement and unable to say no. I felt without seeing the subservience in his eyes, and noticed how his lips trembled; I knew that he wanted to talk to me, but in my daze, where the curiosity of my heart mingled uncertainly with physical numbness, I did nothing to encourage or discourage him. He cleared his throat several times, I noticed that he was trying and failing to speak, but some kind of cruelty which had, mysteriously, passed from the woman in the bar to me enjoyed watching him wrestle with shame and mental torment, and I did not help him, but let the silence lie black and heavy between us. And our steps, his quietly shuffling like an old man's, mine deliberately firm and decided, as if to escape this dirty world, sounded odd together. I felt the tension between us more strongly all the time; it was a shrill silence now, full of unheard cries, and it already resembled a violin string stretched too taut by the time he at last—and at first with dreadful hesitation—managed to bring out his words.

"You saw … you saw … sir, you saw a strange scene in there. Forgive me … forgive me if I mention it again … but it must seem strange to you … and I must look very ridiculous. That woman, you see … "

He stopped again. Something was constricting his throat. Then his voice sank very low, and he whispered rapidly, "That woman ... she's my wife." I must have given a start of surprise, for he quickly went on as if to apologise. "That's to say, she was my wife ... four or five years ago, it was in Geratzheim back in Hesse where I come from ... sir, I wouldn't like you to think ill of her ... perhaps it's my fault she's like that. She wasn't always ... I ... I tormented her. I took her although she was very poor, she didn't even have any household linen, nothing, nothing at all ... and I'm rich, or that's to say well off ... not rich ... at least, I was then ... and you see, sir, perhaps—she's right there—perhaps I was tight-fisted with money ... but then I always was, sir, before this misfortune ... and my father and mother before me, we all were ... and I worked hard for every *pfennig* ... and she was light-minded, she liked pretty things ... but she was poor, and I was always reproaching her for it ... I shouldn't have done it, I know that now, sir, for she is proud, very proud. You mustn't think she's really the way she makes out ... that's a lie, and she does herself violence only ... only to hurt me, to torment me ... and ... and because she's ashamed. Perhaps she's gone to the bad, but I ... I don't think so, because, sir, she was very good, very good ... "

He wiped his eyes in great agitation and stood still. Instinctively, I looked at him, and he suddenly no longer struck me as ridiculous. I found that I could even ignore his curiously servile manner of speech, the way he kept calling me "sir", as only the lower classes do in Germany. His face was greatly exercised by his internal struggle to put his story into words, and his eyes were fixed as he began walking unsteadily forward again, on the roadway itself, as if there, in the flickering light, he were laboriously reading the tale that so painfully tore its way out of his constricted throat.

"Yes, sir," he uttered now, breathing deeply, and in quite a different voice, a deep voice that seemed to come from a gentler world within him, "yes, she was very good ... to me too, she was very grateful to me for saving her from poverty... and I knew that she was grateful, too, but ... but I wanted to hear her say so ... again and again, again and again ... it did me good to hear her thank me ... sir, it was so good, so very good, to feel ... to feel that you are a better human being, when ... when you know all the same that you're not ... I'd have given all my money to hear it again and again ... and she was very proud, so when she realised that I was insisting she must be grateful, she wanted to say so less and less. That's why... that, sir, is the only reason why I always made her ask ... I never gave anything of my own free will ... I felt good, making her come to beg for every dress, every ribbon ... I tormented her like that for three years, I tormented her more and more ... but it was only because I loved her, sir ... I liked her pride, yet I still wanted to make her bow to me, madman that I was, and when she wanted something I was angry ... but I wasn't really, sir ... I was glad of any chance to humiliate her, for ... for I didn't know how much I loved her ... "

He stopped again. He was staggering as he walked now, and had obviously forgotten me. He spoke mechanically, as if in his sleep, in a louder and louder voice.

"And I didn't know ... I didn't know it until that dreadful day when ... when I'd refused to give her money for her mother, only a very little money ... that is, I had it ready for her, but I wanted her to come and ask me once again ... oh, what am I saying? ... yes, I knew then, when I came home in the evening and she was gone, leaving just a note on the table ... 'Keep your damned money, I want no more to do with you,' it said ... nothing more ... sir, I was like a lunatic for three days and three nights. I had the river searched and the woods, I gave the police large sums of money, I went to all the neighbours, but they just laughed and mocked me ... there was no trace of her, nothing. At last a man came with news from the next village ... he said he'd seen her ... in the train with a soldier, she'd gone to Berlin. I followed her that very day ... I neglected my business, I lost thousands ... they stole from me, my servants, my manager, all of them ... but I swear to you,

sir, it was all the same to me … I stayed in Berlin, I stayed
there a week until I found her among all those people …
and went to her … " He was breathing heavily.

"Sir, I swear to you … I didn't say a harsh word to her
… I wept, I went on my knees … I offered her money,
all my fortune, said she should control it, because then I
knew … I knew I couldn't live without her. I love every
hair on her head … her mouth … her body, everything,
everything … and I was the one who thrust her out, I
alone … She was pale as death when I suddenly came
in … I'd bribed the woman she was staying with … a
procuress, a bad, vicious woman … she looked white as
chalk standing there by the wall … she heard me out.
Sir, I believe she was … yes, I think she was almost glad
to see me, but when I mentioned the money … and I
did so, I promise you, only to show her that I wasn't
thinking of it any more … then she spat … and then …
because I still wouldn't go … then she called her lover,
and they both laughed at me … But, sir, I went back
again day after day. The people of the house told me
everything, I knew that the rascal had left her and she
was in dire need, so I went once again … once again,
sir, but she flew at me and tore up a banknote that I'd
secretly left on the table, and when I next came back she
was gone … What didn't I do, sir, to find her again? For
a year, I swear to you, I didn't live, I just kept looking
for her, I paid detective agencies until at last I found out

that she was in Argentina … in … in a house of ill repute … " He hesitated a moment. The last words were spoken like a death rattle. And his voice grew deeper yet.

"I was horrified … at first … but then I remembered that it was I, no one else, who had sent her there … and I thought how she must be suffering, the poor creature … for more than anything else she's proud … I went to my lawyer, who wrote to the consul and sent money … not telling her who it came from … just so that she would come back. I received a telegram to say it had all succeeded … I knew what the ship was, and I waited to meet it in Amsterdam … I was there three days early, burning with impatience … at last it came in, I was so happy just to see the smoke of the steamer on the horizon, and I thought I couldn't wait for it to come in and tie up, so slowly, so slowly, and then the passengers came down the gangplank and at last, at last she was there … I didn't know her at first … she was different, her face painted … and as … as you saw her … and when she saw me waiting … she went pale. Two sailors had to hold her up or she'd have fallen off the gangplank. As soon as she was on shore I came up to her … I said nothing, my throat was too dry … She said nothing either, and didn't look at me … The porter carried her bags, we walked and walked … Then, suddenly, she stopped and said …oh, sir, how she said it … 'Do you still want me for your wife, even now?' I took her hand ... she was trembling, but she said nothing. Yet I felt that everything was all right again ... sir, how happy I was! I danced around her like a child when I had her in the room, I fell at her feet ... I must have said foolish things ... for she laughed through her tears and caressed me ... very hesitantly, of course ... but sir ... it did me so much good. My heart was overflowing. I ran upstairs, downstairs, ordered a dinner in the hotel ... our wedding feast ... I helped her to dress ... and we went down, we ate and drank and made merry ... oh, she was so cheerful, like a child, so warm and good-hearted, and she talked of home ... and how we would see to everything again ... And then ... " His voice suddenly roughened, and he made a movement with his hand as if to knock someone down. "There ... there was a waiter ... a bad, dishonest man ... who thought I was drunk because I was raving and dancing and laughing madly ... although it was just that I was happy, oh, so happy. And then, when I paid him, he gave me back my change twenty francs short ... I shouted at him and demanded the rest ... he was embarrassed, and brought out the money ... And then she began laughing aloud again. I stared at her, but her face was different ... mocking, hard, hostile all at once. 'How pernickety you still are ... even on our wedding day!' she said very coldly, so sharply, with such ... such pity. I was horrified, and cursed myself for being so punctilious … I went to great pains to laugh again, but her merriment was gone, had died. She demanded a room of her own … what wouldn't I have given her? … and I lay alone all night, thinking of nothing but what I could buy her next morning … what I could give her … how to show her that I'm not miserly … would never be miserly with her again. And in the morning I went out, I bought a bracelet, very early, and when I went into her room … it … it was empty, just the same as before. And I knew there'd be a note on the table … I went away and prayed to God it wasn't true … but … but it was there … And it said … " Here he hesitated. Instinctively, I had stopped and was looking at him. He bent his head. Then he whispered, hoarsely:

"It said … 'Leave me alone. I find you repulsive.' "

We had reached the harbour, and suddenly the roar of the nearby breakers broke the silence. There lay the ships at anchor, near and far, lights winking like the eyes of large black animals, and from somewhere came the sound of singing. Nothing was distinct, yet there was so much to feel, an immensity of sleep, with the seaport dreaming deeply.

I sensed the man's shadow beside me, a flickering, spectral shape at my feet, now disintegrating, now coming together again as the light of the dim street lamps changed. I could say nothing, I could give no comfort and had no questions, but I felt his silence clinging to me, heavy and oppressive. Then, suddenly, he clutched my arm. He was trembling.

"But I won't leave this place without her … I've found her again, after months … She torments me, but I won't give up … I beg you, sir, talk to her … I must have her, tell her that, she won't listen to me … I can't go on living like this … I can't watch the men going in to her … and wait outside the house until they come down again, drunk and laughing … The whole alley knows me now, they laugh when they see me waiting … it drives me mad … and yet I go back again every evening. Sir, I beg you, speak to her … I don't know you, but do it for God's merciful sake … speak to her … "

Instinctively, and with horror, I tried to free my arm. But as he felt my resistance to his unhappiness, he suddenly fell on his knees in the middle of the road and embraced my feet.

"I beg you, sir … you must speak to her … you must, or … or something terrible will happen. I've spent all I have looking for her, and I won't … I won't leave her here alive. I've bought a knife … I have a knife, sir … I won't leave her here alive, I can't bear it … Speak to her, sir … "

He was rolling about on the ground in front of me like a madman. At that moment two police officers came down the street. I violently wrenched him up and to his feet. He stared at me for a moment, astonished. Then he said in a dry and very different voice, "Turn down that side-street, and you'll see your hotel." Once more he stared at me with eyes whose pupils seemed to have merged into something terribly white and empty. Then he walked away.

I wrapped my coat around me. I was shivering. I felt nothing but exhaustion, I was in a confused daze, black and devoid of any emotion, a darkly moving slumber. I wanted to think all this over, but that black wave of weariness kept rising inside me, carrying me away. I staggered into the hotel, fell into bed, and slept as soundly as a brute beast.

Next morning I didn't know how much of it all had been a dream and how much was real, and something in me didn't want to know. I had woken late, a stranger in a strange town, and I went to look at a church where there were said to be some very famous mosaics dating from the days of classical antiquity. But I stared blankly at them. Last night's encounter rose more and more clearly before my mind's eye, and I felt an irresistible urge to go in search of that alley and that house. But those strange alleys come to life only at night; by day they wear cold, grey disguises, and only those who know them well can recognise them. However hard I looked, I couldn't find the alley. I came back tired and disappointed, pursued by images of something that was either memory or delusion.

The time of my train was nine in the evening. I left the

town with regret. A porter fetched my bags and carried them to the station for me. On our way, I suddenly turned at a crossing; I recognised the alley leading to the house, told the porter to wait, and—while he smiled first in surprise, then knowingly—went to look at the scene of my adventure once more.

There it lay in the dark, as dark as yesterday, and in the faint moonlight I saw the glass pane in the house door gleaming. Once again I was going closer when, with a rustling sound, a figure emerged from the darkness. With a shudder, I saw him waiting there in the doorway and beckoning me to approach. Dread took hold of me—I fled quickly, in cowardly fear of getting involved here and missing my train.

But then, just before I turned the corner of the alley, I looked back once again. When my gaze fell on him he pulled himself together and strode to the door. He quickly opened his hand, and I saw the glint of metal in it. From a distance, I couldn't tell whether the moonlight showed money or a knife gleaming there in his fingers …

Jeanne Agnès Berthelot de Plémont, Marquise de Prie (1698-1727)
Attributed to Louis Michel van Loo

AFTERWORD

These two stories by Stefan Zweig appear superficially very different in theme, yet both examine a subject which clearly fascinated him: the human mind in extremis, working its way through a situation of intense personal crisis. *Twilight*, the longer novella, also reflects Zweig's interest in French history and literature. He was a noted Francophile who felt that France was in many ways his spiritual home, and wrote a number of historical biographies, including one of Marie Antoinette. His studies of literary figures include several French writers and his special affinity with France is evident in this story, along with his knowledge of the country's history.

His central figure, Madame de Prie—who really existed—was the mistress of Louis XV's prime minister the Duke of Bourbon, and did indeed (as Zweig tells us) help to arrange the young king's marriage to Marie Leszczynska, daughter of the exiled king of Poland. Madame de Prie's portrait was painted by the French artist Louis Michel Van Loo, and as Zweig also mentions, she had a play dedicated to her by Voltaire no less. It is also historical fact that she committed suicide in 1727, after being exiled to her country estate. I think we may assume that the details of her psychological decline in this story are Zweig's, as he traces the career of a woman used to pulling the strings of power who disintegrates once they are snatched from her grasp. From a hopeful belief that she may yet be back in favour at court some day, his heroine passes to a state of hysterical desperation in which she clutches at emotional straws, and then elaborately stages her own suicide with delusional elation. At the same time Zweig presents a vignette of high society in the France of the early eighteenth century, a century which was of course to end with the French Revolution.

By way of contrast, *Moonbeam Alley* is a shorter tale of purely private passions, yet is equally tense and anguished. The narrator of the framework story, delayed for an extra day in a small French seaport, is nostalgically reminded of his native Germany by hearing a woman singing an aria from Weber's Romantic opera *Der Freischütz,* and as a spectator becomes drawn into the heavily charged atmosphere of a human tragedy. As in several of Zweig's other novellas, for instance *Twenty-Four Hours in the Life of a Woman* and *Amok,* the narrator's function is to elicit confidences from the real protagonist of the story, in this case a man whose thrifty (or avaricious) instincts have lost him the love of the wife he plucked from poverty, yet whom he still loves. Their doomed relationship is disclosed to the delayed traveller who has been drawn to the bar where the woman now works as a prostitute, while she rejects all attempts at reconciliation from her husband, who has followed her there. In only a few pages, Zweig depicts all the pent-up tension of their complex situation, which looks as if it can and will be resolved only by violence.

The framework device is a favourite of Zweig's; the narrator, usually anonymous, is not personally involved in the story, or only very distantly so, but hears the central character recount his or her own tale. Alternatively he may, as in *Fantastic Night,* be the recipient of papers which he is to publish. The protagonists themselves, however, recount tales of acute moral or emotional dilemmas. Zweig was extremely interested in Freudian psychology, and much as Freud recorded case histories which he made literary works in themselves, Zweig employs the most meticulous of language to tell his fictional tales of characters in states of heightened emotional awareness.